For Sailor,

who's always by my side.

For more books by Victoria Scudder visit:

Sweet Baby Pink

A rhyming book for little girls

by Victoria Scudder

Scout & Company Publishing

Pink boat,
sailboat,
what do you see?

I see a seagull
soaring near me.

Little bird,
blue bird,
what do you see?

I see a dinosaur
looking at me.

Sweet bunny,
pink bunny,
what do you see?

I see a balloon
lifting up me.

Baby penguin,
little penguin,
what do you see?

I see my parents
watching over me.

Red truck,
rosie truck,
what do you see?

I see raindrops
falling on me.

Crescent moon,
sleepy moon,
what do you see?

I see stars
twinkling near me.

Mother earth,
green earth,
what do you see?

I see an astronaut
floating by me.

Summer daisy,
pink daisy,
what do you see?

I see a bunny rabbit
hiding from me.

Flamingo bird,
tall bird,
what do you see?

I see a beach ball
bouncing near me.

Baby chick,
yellow chick,
what do you see?

I see a ballerina
dancing for me.

Yellow bee,
bumblebee,
what do you see?

I see butterflies
fluttering by me.

Watermelon,
summer melon,
what do you see?

I see strawberries
next to me.

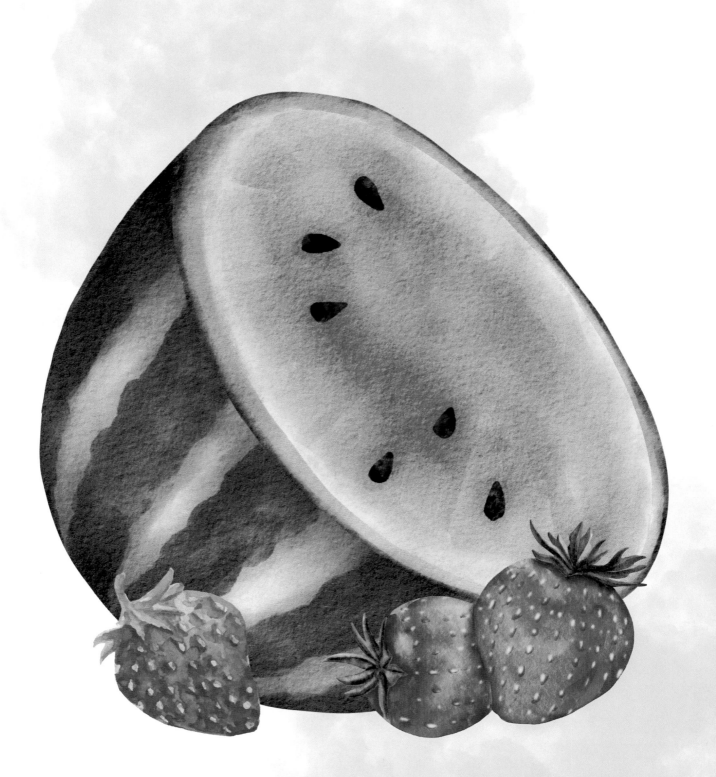

Green turtle,
sea turtle,
what do you see?

I see a jellyfish
swimming by me.

Unicycle,
single cycle,
what do you see?

I see a panda bear
riding on me.

About the Author

Victoria is an internationally award-winning and best-selling children's book author and independent publisher with 15 years of classroom teaching experience in K-8th grade.

Please sign up for my newsletter at www.Victoria-Scudder.com. I promise not to bombard you, and I'll always make it fun!

For impromptu updates, visit www.facebook.com/scoutandcompanypublishing/.

Author website: www.Victoria-Scudder.com

I hope you enjoyed reading *Sweet Baby Pink* as much as I had fun creating it. I'd love to hear from you at scoutandcompanyflorida@gmail.com!

Want more Sweet Baby? Check out the rest of the series!

Please leave a review

Your **review** means a LOT to me! Please take a moment to <u>log into</u> **<u>Amazon</u>** <u>and review my book</u>. This helps *Sweet Baby Pink* get seen! Make a baby happy - spread the word!

P.S. I'm fully aware that many boys like pink too! But this book just happens to be for the girls.

Scan Here

Made in the USA
Middletown, DE
21 October 2024

62974604R00020